D0524674

TREASURED TALES OF CHILDHOOD

All-Time Favorites

Put together by
Barbara Simons and Ruth Rooney

Published by THE SOUTHWESTERN COMPANY Nashville, Tennessee

All-Time Favorites

Contents

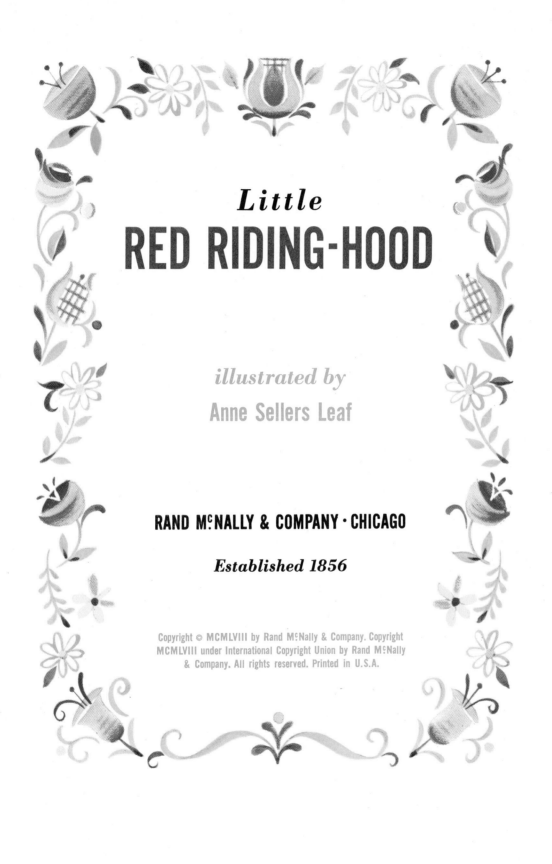

Little
RED RIDING-HOOD

illustrated by

Anne Sellers Leaf

RAND McNALLY & COMPANY · CHICAGO

Established 1856

ONCE UPON A TIME there was a little
village girl who was as sweet as sugar and
as good as bread. Her mother loved her very
much, and her grandmother was even fonder

of her. This kind grandmother had made her a pretty red cloak with a hood, in which the child looked so bright and gay that everyone called her Little Red Riding-Hood.

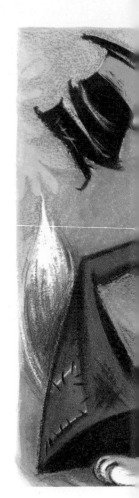

One day her mother made some cakes and said to her, "Go, my child, and see how your grandmother is. I hear she has been ill. Take her one of these cakes and this little pot of butter."

So Little Red Riding-Hood set out at once to see her grandmother, who lived in another village.

As she walked through the woods she met a big wolf. He would have gobbled her up then and there, but some woodcutters were

near by and he did not dare. But he did ask
her where she was going. The little girl did
not know it was dangerous to talk to a wolf,
and so she said,

"I am going to my grandmother, to take
her this cake and little pot of butter."

"Does she live far off?" asked the wolf.

"Oh, yes," answered Little Red Riding-
Hood. "She lives beyond the mill you see way
down there, at the first house in the village."

"All right," said the wolf. "I'll go and visit her too. I will take this way, and you take that way, and we'll see who gets there first."

Soon the wolf arrived at the grandmother's cottage and knocked at the door—tap! tap!

"Who is there?"

"It is your own Little Red Riding-Hood," said the wolf, making his voice sound as much like Little Red Riding-Hood's as he could.

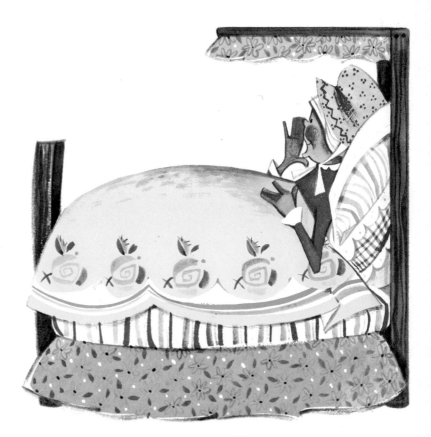

The good old woman, who wasn't feeling well and so was in bed, called out, "Pull the string, my dear, and the latch will fly up."

The wolf pulled the string and the door opened. He sprang upon the poor old grandmother and swallowed her all in one gulp, for it was more than three days since he had had a bite. He did not feel very well after that, but he shut the door, put on the grandmother's cap, and stretched himself out in the old woman's bed to wait for Little Red Riding-Hood.

By and by Little Red Riding-Hood came knocking at the cottage door—tap! tap!
"Who is there?"

At first Little Red Riding-Hood was frightened at the hoarse voice of the wolf. But she made up her mind that her grandmother must have a cold.

"It is your own Little Red Riding-Hood," she answered. "I have brought you a cake and a little pot of butter which Mother has made and sent you."

Then the wolf called out, softening his voice as well as he could, "Pull the string, my dear, and the latch will fly up."

Little Red Riding-Hood pulled the string and the door opened.

When the wolf saw her come in, he hid himself under the bedclothes and said,

"Put the cake and the little pot of butter on the shelf, and come here."

And so Little Red Riding-Hood put the cake and butter on the shelf and went over to the wolf. She was very much surprised to see how strange her grandmother looked in her night clothes and said,

"Grandmother, what great arms you have!"
"The better to hug you, my child!"
"Grandmother, what great ears you have!"
"The better to hear you, my child!"
"Grandmother, what great eyes you have!"
"The better to see you, my child!"
"Grandmother, what great teeth you have!"
"The better to eat you!"

With these words the wicked wolf fell upon poor Little Red Riding-Hood.

And there the story ends. Nobody knows just what happened. Some say that the woodsmen were so near by, cutting trees, that they heard Little Red Riding-Hood scream and came running, just in time to save her. And they say, too, that when the woodsmen cut the wolf open, there they found the grandmother, whole and sound!

Sleeping Beauty

Illustrated by
ELIZABETH WEBBE

RAND McNALLY
& COMPANY

Chicago · *Established 1856*

ONCE UPON A TIME there lived a King and Queen who had long wished for a child. And when one day a sweet daughter was born to them the King was so happy that he gave a great christening

feast. As godmothers for his little daughter he
asked the seven good fairies in the kingdom. The
one bad-tempered fairy was not invited.

After the christening there was a splendid
feast. Before each fairy was placed an emerald
plate, like a clover leaf, set with diamond dew-
drops. Suddenly the one uninvited fairy rode into
the hall on a dragonfly, muttering threats.

Now the fairies, as was their custom, began to give their gifts to the Princess. The youngest gave her beauty; the next wit; the third, grace; the fourth, virtue; the fifth, a lovely voice; the sixth, a smile to win all hearts.

Then the uninvited, bad-tempered fairy cried out, "The King's daughter in her rosebud youth shall prick her hand with a spindle, and fall down dead!"

Everybody started to cry out, but then the seventh fairy popped up from behind the cradle and said, "Be comforted, O King and Queen! My gift is still to come. I cannot undo entirely what this unkind fairy has done.

"Your daughter will prick her hand with the spindle, but instead of dying she will sink into a deep sleep which will last a hundred years. From that sleep, when her dream is over, a king's son shall waken her."

Yet the King hoped to save his dear child from the threatened evil. He had his heralds proclaim that no one in all the country should have a spindle in the house.

One day when the Princess was fifteen years old, she went roaming about the palace, exploring

one room after another. At last she came to a
little room at the top of the tower. There an old
woman sat busily spinning, as she had never
heard of the King's proclamation.

"Good day, Granny!" said the Princess. "What
are you doing?"

"I am spinning, my pretty lass," said the
old woman. "Would you like to try it?"

"Oh, yes," the Princess cried. But when she
caught at the whirling spindle it pricked her hand.
She fell back in a faint.

The old woman, greatly alarmed, cried for
help. People came running from all sides.

The King and Queen knew at once the fairy's
evil wish had been fulfilled. They had the Princess

carried to a room deep in the heart of the palace, and laid on a bed decked with green and gold covers. The King sadly commanded that she be left to sleep in peace until the hour of her awakening had come to pass.

Now the wise fairy, whose quick wit had saved the life of the Princess, knew what had happened and came at once in her swan chariot. She touched with her wand everything and everybody about the palace, except the King and the Queen. She touched the governesses and the ladies in waiting, the gentlemen, the officers, the stewards, cooks, guards, and pages.

As she touched them, they all fell asleep, not to waken until their mistress should wake, and need them to attend her.

The King and Queen kissed their daughter, and left the hushed palace. The King issued a new proclamation, forbidding anyone to approach its gates. But such laws were not needed, for

soon a hedge of thorny shrubs grew around the
palace grounds. They became so thick and high
that neither beast nor man could force a way
through. The castle itself was hidden. Only the
top of the tower could be seen from a distance.

On the day that the hundred years ended, the
son of the king then reigning was a-hunting and
spied the tower beyond the forest. He asked what
it was. An old peasant told him the legend of the
sleeping princess and of the king's son who was to
waken her. From the way the Prince's heart began

beating, he felt certain that the peasant spoke the truth. He knew that he was the king's son who was to waken the princess. He set out at once. The great trees and thorns opened of their own accord to let him pass. And at last the castle stood before him.

He entered the courtyard and saw men and animals in deep slumber. The Prince crossed the court and mounted the stairs.

On he went to the very heart of the palace where, in a beautiful room of gold, he saw the loveliest sight in the world—a sleeping princess,

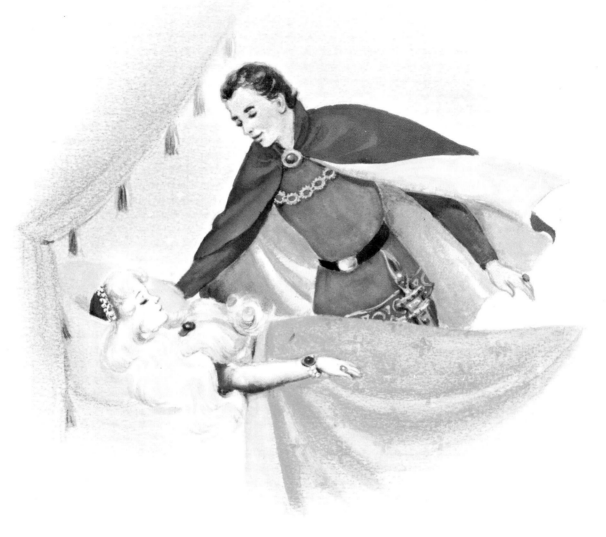

so fair she seemed an angel. He fell on his knees beside her and kissed her lovely cheek.

The Princess opened her eyes, smiled and said, "Is it you, my Prince? I have waited long."

They talked for hours and still had not said half that was in their hearts to say. Meanwhile, everything in the palace waked with the Princess, and everyone took up his task just where he had left it. At nightfall a lady in waiting curtsied to the Princess and announced the wedding feast.

Then the king's son led his bride to the royal chapel, where they were married.

The next morning the bridegroom and bride left the palace and passed through the dark forest into the bright sunshine of the world beyond. And when the Princess turned to look at the castle where she had slept so many years, *behold*, castle and forest had vanished.

So the Princess rode with her Prince to his father's court, and there they lived a life as happy as her dream.

The
Three
Bears

Illustrated by Elizabeth Webbe

RAND McNALLY & COMPANY · Chicago
Established 1856

Once upon a time there were Three Bears who lived in a little house in the woods. One of them was a Little Small Wee Bear, one was a Middle-sized Bear, and one was a Great Big Bear.

They each had a bowl for their porridge. The Little Small Wee Bear had a little tiny bowl, the Middle-sized Bear had a middle-sized bowl, and the Great Big Bear had a great big bowl.

And they each had a chair to sit in. The Little
Small Wee Bear had a little wee chair, the Middle-
sized Bear had a middle-sized chair, and the Great
Big Bear had a great big chair.

And also they each had a bed to sleep in. The
Little Small Wee Bear had a tiny little bed, the
Middle-sized Bear had a middle-sized bed, and
the Great Big Bear had a great huge bed.

One morning, after they had made the porridge for their breakfast and poured it into their porridge bowls, the Three Bears went for a walk in the woods while their porridge cooled, for they did not want to burn their mouths by trying to eat it too soon.

While they were walking in the woods, a little girl whose name was Goldilocks came to the house. She looked in at the window and then she peeped

in at the keyhole and, seeing nobody in the house, she lifted the latch and went in. There she saw the porridge on the table.

First she tasted the porridge of the Great Big Bear, and that was too hot.

Then she tasted the porridge of the Middle-sized Bear, but that was too cold.

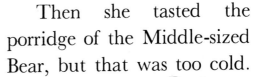

And then she went to the porridge of the Little Small Wee Bear and that was neither too hot nor too cold but just right, and she ate it all up.

Next Goldilocks went into the parlor and there she saw the three chairs. First she tried sitting in the chair of the Great Big Bear, but that was too hard. And then she sat down in the chair of the Middle-sized Bear, but that was too soft. But the chair of the Little Small Wee Bear was just right. And she sat in it until the bottom broke.

Then Goldilocks went into the bedchamber where the Three Bears slept. And first she lay down

upon the bed of the Great Big Bear, but that was
too high at the head for her.

Next she lay down upon the bed of the
Middle-sized Bear, but that was too high at the
foot for her.

And then she lay down upon the bed of the
Little Small Wee Bear, and that was neither too
high at the head nor too high at the foot, but
just right.

So she covered herself up comfortably and fell
fast asleep.

By this time the Three Bears had been walking about for some time in the woods and they thought their porridge would be cool enough now, so they came home to eat their breakfast.

Now Goldilocks had left the spoon of the Great Big Bear standing in his porridge, and he noticed it, first thing.

"SOMEBODY HAS BEEN AT MY POR-RIDGE!" said the Great Big Bear, in his great, rough, gruff voice.

And when the Middle-sized Bear looked at her porridge, she saw that the spoon was standing in her porridge, too.

"SOMEBODY HAS BEEN AT MY POR-RIDGE!" said the Middle-sized Bear, in her middle-sized voice.

Then the Little Small Wee Bear looked at his porridge, and there was the spoon in his bowl also, but the porridge was all gone, every bit.

"SOMEBODY HAS BEEN AT MY PORRIDGE, AND HAS EATEN IT ALL UP!" cried the Little Small Wee Bear, in his little, small, wee voice.

Now Goldilocks had not put the hard cushion straight when she rose from the chair of the Great Big Bear, and when he came into the parlor he noticed it, first thing.

"SOMEBODY HAS BEEN SITTING IN MY CHAIR!" said the Great Big Bear, in his great, rough, gruff voice.

Goldilocks had pushed down the soft cushion in the middle-sized chair.

"*SOMEBODY HAS BEEN SITTING IN MY CHAIR!*" said the Middle-sized Bear, in her middle-sized voice.

"SOMEBODY HAS BEEN SITTING IN MY CHAIR AND HAS SAT THE BOTTOM OUT OF IT!" said the Little Small Wee Bear, in his little, small, wee voice.

Then the Three Bears thought that they had better search through the rest of the house, so they went into the bedchamber where they slept.

Now Goldilocks had pulled the pillow of the Great Big Bear out of its place, and he noticed it, first thing.

"SOMEBODY HAS BEEN LYING IN MY

BED!" said the Great Big Bear in his great, rough, gruff voice.

And Goldilocks had pulled the pillow of the Middle-sized Bear out of its place.

"SOMEBODY HAS BEEN LYING IN MY BED!" said the Middle-sized Bear, in her middle-sized voice.

And when the Little Small Wee Bear came to look at his bed, there was the pillow in its right place, and upon the pillow was the golden-haired Goldilocks.

"SOMEBODY HAS BEEN LYING IN MY BED AND HERE SHE IS!" said the Little Small Wee Bear, in his little, small, wee voice.

When Goldilocks heard the little, small, wee voice of the Little Small Wee Bear, it was so sharp and so shrill that it awakened her at once. Upon seeing the Three Bears she ran to the window, and jumped out.

And whether or not Goldilocks ever found her way out of the woods and became a better little girl, no one has ever known. But the Three Bears never saw her again.

Cinderella

illustrated by
Catherine Barnes

Copyright © 1961 by
WHITMAN PUBLISHING COMPANY
RACINE, WISCONSIN
Printed in the U.S.A. by Western Printing and Lithographing Company

Once upon a time in a faraway city in a distant land, there lived a girl who was good and gentle and beautiful. Her name was Cinderella, and she lived with her proud stepmother and two haughty stepsisters.

All day long Cinderella heard:
"Scrub the floor, Cinderella!"
"Iron my dress, Cinderella!"
"Curl my hair, Cinderella!"

At night Cinderella's stepsisters went off to their beautiful pink satin bedrooms. And Cinderella cried herself to sleep among the cinders by the fire.

One day a messenger from the king announced that a grand ball would take place at the royal palace. All the ladies of the land were invited so that the prince could choose a wife.

"I will be lovely in green velvet and lace," said the first stepsister.

"And I will look very beautiful in purple satin," said the second.

"Cinderella!" screeched their mother. "Start sewing at once!"

Poor Cinderella spent long days making beautiful ball gowns for her stepsisters. And when the evening of the ball came, they put on the lovely gowns and went off without even saying thank you.

Cinderella sat down beside the fire and cried. "Oh, how I wish," she sighed, "how I wish that *I* could —"

"That *you* could go to the ball," said a soft voice. "And so you shall. Fetch me a pumpkin!"

Cinderella looked up. There standing before her was her very own fairy god-mother. Cinderella dried her tears and hurried to find the biggest pumpkin in the garden.

A wave of her fairy godmother's wand, and the pumpkin became a coach, a golden coach with silver doors and soft velvet seats.

Another wave of the wand, and six white mice became six prancing white horses.

With still another wave of the magic wand a great rat became a tall coachman and two tiny green lizards became footmen. And then . . .

and then Cinderella's fairy godmother
touched Cinderella herself with the wonderful wand. In a twinkling she felt
something soft as a cloud drift down
about her shoulders, and found that she
was wearing a silky white gown. On her
feet were sparkling glass slippers.

Her fairy godmother helped Cinderella into the coach. "*Be sure,*" she said, "*that you are home by midnight!*" And then, with a "HI-YUP!" from the coachman, Cinderella rode off in splendor to the royal palace.

When Cinderella arrived at the ball the prince asked her to dance. The other guests watched and wondered who this beautiful princess could be!

The evening grew late. Cinderella was so happy dancing with the prince that she forgot her fairy godmother's warning. She forgot that she must be home by midnight. She *forgot,* that is, until . . .

Bong! Bong! Bong! The clock began to strike. Cinderella looked up and saw that the hands pointed to midnight.

Bong! Bong! Bong!
She ran from the
ballroom.

Bong! Bong! Bong!
Her feet scarcely
touched the stairs
of the great wide
staircase that led to
the palace.

Bong! Bong! Bong! Cinderella reached the road just as the clock stopped striking. And there waiting for her were — a broken pumpkin, and six white mice, and a large gray rat, and two very tiny green lizards!

Looking down she found herself wearing her old brown rags. One of the glass slippers still gleamed on her foot, though. Gently she took it off and tucked it into her pocket. Then she started for home.

And the prince, who had come to look for Cinderella, found only a tiny glass slipper lying on the great staircase.

"I must find my lovely princess," he said. And so he sent one of the king's messengers to try the glass slipper on every lady in the land, saying that he would marry whoever the slipper fit.

The messenger traveled the length and breadth of the kingdom. At last he reached the home of Cinderella and her stepsisters.

Cinderella's stepsisters pushed and pulled, hobbled and hopped, trying to squeeze their great feet into the tiny slipper. But anyone could see that the shoe had never been worn by them.

The king's messenger looked about and saw Cinderella seated before the

fire. Her stepsisters giggled behind their
hands as he bowed before her. But they
gasped as he placed the glass slipper on
her foot. And as her amazed stepsisters
watched, Cinderella took the other slipper from her pocket and slipped it onto
her other foot.

With that Cinderella's fairy godmother appeared. She touched Cinderella with her magic wand, and Cinderella
was dressed once more in a dainty white
gown. On her head rested a sparkling
jeweled crown.

The king's messenger helped her into
the king's coach, and they drove away
to the royal palace.

And there lovely Cinderella and her
handsome prince were married and lived
most happily ever after.

PUSS-IN-BOOTS

Illustrations by
BERNICE & LOU MYERS

RAND McNALLY
& COMPANY · Chicago

ONCE UPON A TIME a miller died and left all he possessed to his three sons. But he had only these three things—his mill, his ass, and his cat.

The property was soon divided. The eldest brother took the mill. The second son received the ass. That left only the cat for the youngest, who could not be comforted for his bad luck.

"My brothers," said he, "will be able to earn a living, if they work together. But when I have eaten my cat, and made a fur collar of his skin, I shall die of hunger!"

The cat had heard all this. Coming up to his new master, he said, "Do not worry, Master. Give me a hempen sack, and have me made a pair of boots, so that the brambles may not tear my feet. You shall see that you have not fared so badly."

As soon as the cat had got what he asked for, he put on his fine new boots and hung the sack around his neck. Then he went off to the rabbit meadow. Inside the bag he put some bran.

Hardly had he lain down
when a reckless young rabbit ran into the sack.

The cat now went to the King. He was shown
the way to the King's audience chamber. Making
a fine low bow to the King, he said, "Sire, here is
a rabbit which my lord, the Marquis of Carabas,
has bidden me bring you."

"Say 'thank you' to your master, and tell him
I am much pleased," said the King.

A few days later the cat hid in a wheat field. This time two partridges walked into his bag. At once he drew tight the strings, and the birds were safely caught. These he presented to the King, as he had presented the rabbit. The King was delighted and gave orders that the cat should be given something good to eat.

Thus the cat kept on for two or three months.

One day he learned that the next morning the King was going to drive on the banks of the mill stream with his daughter, who was the most beautiful princess in the whole world. So the cat said to his owner, "If you will take my advice, your fortune is made. You have only to go bathing in the stream. I will show you where."

The cat's master could not see what good could come of that. Still, he did as Puss advised.

While he was enjoying his bath, the King passed by. Now what did Sir Cat do but begin to cry with all his might, "Help! help! The most honorable Marquis of Carabas is drowning!"

The King put his royal head outside the curtains of his carriage. As soon as he recognized the cat, he commanded his royal guard to run in haste to the aid of the most honorable Marquis of Carabas.

While they were dragging the Marquis out of the water, the cat drew near the royal coach. He told the King that thieves had come and carried away all his master's clothes. Now it was really the cat himself who had hidden them.

The King ordered his Royal Wardrobe Keeper to go and fetch some of his finest garments for the most honorable Marquis.

The fine clothing set off his good looks so very well that the King's daughter found him exceedingly to her taste. The Marquis of Carabas had no sooner looked at her two or three times than he liked her very much indeed. The King, noting this, asked the Marquis to join the royal party on its drive.

The cat went running ahead. On meeting some peasants who were mowing he said to them, "Good folk who mow, if you do not tell the King that this meadow belongs to the most honorable Marquis of Carabas, you shall be minced as fine as pie meat!"

When the King passed, he asked the mowers whose meadow they were mowing. "It belongs to the Marquis of Carabas," they all said, for they were frightened by the cat's warning.

"You have a noble inheritance," said the King to the Marquis.

At last Puss reached a great castle. The owner was an Ogre. He was the richest Ogre you ever saw, for all the lands through which the King had passed really belonged to him. The cat had taken pains to find out what special magic the Ogre could do. Now he asked if he could speak with the owner of the castle.

"I've been told," said Sir Cat to the Ogre, "that you can change yourself into any sort of animal—for instance, into a lion, or even into an elephant!"

"That is true," said the Ogre, crossly, "and to prove it you shall see me change into a lion!"

Puss was so frightened to see a real lion in front of him that he reached the roof in the twinkling of an eye and climbed out upon the gutters for greater safety.

When Puss saw that the Ogre had changed back again, he came down from the roof. He confessed to the Ogre that he had had a very great fright.

"I've also been told," said Puss, "that you can take the shape of the very tiniest animal; for example, a rat, or even a mouse. I'll admit that I think it quite impossible."

"Impossible!" roared the Ogre. "You shall see for yourself!" And instantly he changed into a mouse and began to run about upon the floor. No sooner did the eyes of Puss-in-Boots fall upon the mouse than he threw himself upon it and ate it up!

Now the King, as he passed by, noticed the mighty castle of the Ogre and wished to visit it. Puss-in-Boots ran out to meet the royal party. "Welcome, Your Majesty!" he said. "Welcome to the castle of the most honorable Marquis of Carabas!"

"How is this, Marquis?" cried the King. "This wonderful palace, too, is yours? Nothing can be lovelier than this courtyard. Let us see the inside, I pray you."

Following His Majesty, who entered first, they all went into the great hall. There they found

ready a luncheon which the Ogre had ordered to be prepared for friends.

After seeing the immense wealth of the Marquis, and having drunk his health, the King said to him, "There is no one, my dear Marquis, whom I should like better as my son-in-law. It rests only with you."

The Marquis, with a low bow, accepted joyfully the honor offered him by the King.

As for Puss-in-Boots, he became a great lord and hunted mice only when he wanted amusement.

The Night
Before Christmas
By
Clement C. Moore
Pictures by Charles Clement

Copyright, MCMLV, by
WHITMAN PUBLISHING COMPANY
RACINE, WISCONSIN
Printed in the U.S.A. by Western Printing
and Lithographing Company

'T WAS the night before Christmas
when all through the house
Not a creature was stirring,
not even a mouse.

The stockings were hung
by the chimney with care
In hopes that St. Nicholas
soon would be there.

The children were nestled all snug in their beds,

While visions of sugarplums danced in their heads.

And Mamma in her kerchief and I in my cap

Had just settled down for a long winter's nap,

When out on the lawn
    there arose such a clatter,
I sprang from my bed
    to see what was the matter.
Away to the window
    I flew like a flash,
Tore open the shutters
    and threw up the sash.

The moon on the breast
    of the new-fallen snow
Gave a luster of midday
    to objects below.

When, what to my
    wondering eyes should appear,
But a miniature sleigh
    and eight tiny reindeer,
With a little old driver
    so lively and quick,
I knew in a moment
    it must be Saint Nick.

"Now, Dasher! Now, Dancer!
Now, Prancer and Vixen!
On, Comet! On, Cupid!
On, Donner and Blitzen!
To the top of the porch,
to the top of the wall!
Now, dash away! Dash away!
Dash away, all!"

More rapid than eagles
his coursers they came,
And he whistled and shouted
and called them by name:

As dry leaves that before the wild hurricane fly,
When they meet with an obstacle, mount to the sky,
So up to the housetop the coursers they flew
With a sleigh full of toys and St. Nicholas too.
And then in a twinkling I heard on the roof
The prancing and pawing of each little hoof.

As I drew in my head
    and was turning around,
Down the chimney
    Saint Nicholas came
    with a bound.
He was dressed
    all in fur from
    his head to his foot,
And his clothes
    were all tarnished
    with ashes and soot.

A bundle of toys he had
    flung on his back,
And he looked like a peddler
    just opening his pack.
His eyes—how they twinkled!
    His dimples—how merry!
His cheeks were like roses,
    his nose like a cherry.
His droll little mouth
    was drawn up like a bow,
And the beard on his chin
    was as white as the snow.

The stump of a pipe
   he held tight in his teeth,
And the smoke
   it encircled his head
   like a wreath.
He had a broad face
   and a round little belly
That shook when he laughed
   like a bowl full of jelly.
He was chubby and plump,
   a right jolly old elf,
And I laughed
   when I saw him
   in spite of myself.
A wink of his eye
   and a twist of his head
Soon gave me to know
   I had nothing to dread.

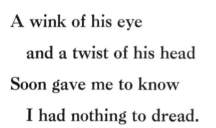

He spoke not a word but went straight to his work,
And filled all the stockings; then turned with a jerk,
And laying his finger aside of his nose,
And giving a nod, up the chimney he rose.

He sprang to his sleigh, to his team gave a whistle,

And away they all flew like the down of a thistle.

But I heard him exclaim ere he drove out of sight,

"Happy Christmas to all and to all

The Gingerbread Man

Illustrated by Anne Sellers Leaf

RAND McNALLY & COMPANY
Chicago • *Established 1856*

ONCE UPON A TIME a little old man and a little old woman lived in a pleasant cottage behind a white fence. They were very happy, for their grandchildren lived nearby.

One day the little old woman was baking. When she had put her loaves of bread into the oven, she said to herself, "Now I shall make some gingerbread cookies for my grandchildren."

So she made a lot of gingerbread cookies. She put them into a pan, and put the pan into the oven to bake.

"I have some gingerbread dough left," she said to herself. "I know what I'll do. I shall make a little Gingerbread Man." So she rolled out the dough, and very cleverly she shaped a little Gingerbread Man.

"Now to dress him up," said the little old woman. She sprinkled brown sugar over his round little body to give him a brown coat, and she stuck three big raisins in front for buttons. Then she gave him a pair of raisins for eyes and a little lump of gingerbread for a nose. His mouth she made with pink sugar.

She was pleased with him, and said,

"Ah, there, my little Gingerbread Man,
Now you're all ready to go to the pan."

So in a pan she laid him, and popped him into the oven. Then she went on about her work while the fire burned and the oven baked the little Gingerbread Man.

At last she opened the oven door.

"My goodness, what a fine Gingerbread Man!" cried the little old woman when she saw what a wonderful brown color he was. "I'll just lay him in the cupboard to cool, and when the children come, they can eat him."

But when the little Gingerbread Man heard this, he jumped up in the shiny pan and hopped right out onto the clean kitchen floor.

"No one shall eat me!" he cried, and ran toward the door on his sturdy legs, shouting,

"I can run away from you, I can.
'Cause I'm the little Gingerbread Man!"

The little old woman was so surprised she didn't know what to do.

"Stop! Stop!" she called.

But the little Gingerbread Man ran on into
the yard. Out in the garden the little old man
was hoeing. When he saw the Gingerbread Man,
he dropped his hoe and ran after him.

"Stop! Stop!" he cried, but the Gingerbread
Man wouldn't stop.

He darted out through the gate in the white
fence, shouting,

"I can run away from you, I can.
'Cause I'm the little Gingerbread Man!"

And he ran down the road so fast that the little
old man was left far behind.

On and on he ran, and after a while he met a big black dog.

"Stop!" cried the dog. "Stop, and I'll take you home for my puppies to play with!"

But the little Gingerbread Man just laughed and called back,

"I can run away from you, I can.
I ran from the little old woman,
And the little old man.
And *you* can't catch me,
'Cause I'm the little Gingerbread Man!"

Nor could the big black dog catch him, though she ran until she was tired.

After a while the little Gingerbread Man met
a big yellow cow.

"Stop!" she cried. "Stop, and let my little
calf play with you!"

But he just laughed, and called back, "If
you can catch me, I'll stop!"

The cow, however, was too wise to run after
him, and soon he had left her far behind.

At last the Gingerbread Man ran past a big tall horse. The horse jumped a fence and ran along the road, too. He ran so fast—*rackety-rackety-rackety!*—that he soon caught up, and the little Gingerbread Man was frightened. But the horse said,

"This is the best race I ever ran!
What a runner you are,
Little Gingerbread Man!"

For the big tall horse just wanted to race.
And after a while, he turned back, saying,

"Run along, run along,
   Little Gingerbread Man,
   But beware of the fox,
   For he'll catch you if he can!"

So the little Gingerbread Man ran on alone,
and thought what a fine fellow the horse was.

And at last the little Gingerbread Man ran around a turn in the road—and who should be sitting there but the fox!

"Good day," called the fox. "What a runner you are! You must be tired from running so much."

But little Gingerbread Man stopped. Now that he thought of it, his sturdy gingerbread legs *were* getting tired.

"My house is quite near," the fox told him, "and you can rest there, and eat dinner with me, too. Running must have made you hungry."

Now that he thought of it, the little Gingerbread Man *was* hungry. "How kind you are, Mr. Fox," he said.

"Just follow me, then," smiled the fox. And he led the way with the tired Gingerbread Man following at his heels.

"What a treat he will make for my little ones!" thought the fox. "They will lick the sugar from his coat, and pick out his raisin eyes, and then gobble him down." But of course he didn't say a word of this out loud.

When they were almost at the fox's house, a bird in a treetop saw them coming and sang out,

"Run! run! little Gingerbread Man,
For the fox will eat you if he can!"

Then the little Gingerbread Man stopped in his tracks and remembered what the big tall horse had said. "If you want to eat me," he called, "you must catch me first!" And away he ran, with the fox right after him.

But the little Gingerbread Man could run much
faster, and he shouted,

"I can run away from you, I can.
I ran away from the little old woman,
And the little old man,
And a big black dog,
And a big yellow cow.
As fast as the big tall horse I ran.
And *you* can't catch me,
'Cause I'm the little Gingerbread Man!"

He ran on and on, and left the angry fox far behind. Past the big tall horse he ran, and past the big yellow cow, and the big black dog. When he came to the cottage of the little old man and the little old woman, he was very tired.

Just as he neared the white fence, a little girl and boy came through the gate. They were the grandchildren.

"Why, here's the Gingerbread Man that Grandmother baked for us!" they cried. "Let's catch him!" And after him they ran.

The little Gingerbread Man was glad. "I'll be good, and let them catch me," he said to himself. "These are the children I was made for, and they shall have me, after all."

So the little Gingerbread Man ran so slowly that the children soon caught him. This was the best fate that could befall the little Gingerbread Man, don't you think?